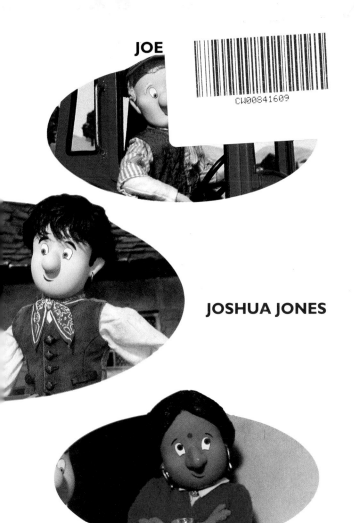

JOE

JOSHUA JONES

MRS KARIA

MEET ALL THESE FRIENDS IN BUZZ BOOKS:

Thomas the Tank Engine
Fireman Sam
Looney Tunes
Bugs Bunny
Toucan 'Tecs
Barney
Police Academy
Flintstones
Jetsons
Joshua Jones

First published 1992 by Buzz Books,
an imprint of Reed International Books Ltd,
Michelin House, 81 Fulham Road, London SW3 6RB

LONDON MELBOURNE AUCKLAND

Joshua Jones film © 1990 S4C
Joshua Jones character © 1989 Rob Lee
Text © 1992 William Heinemann Ltd
Illustrations © 1992 William Heinemann Ltd
Based on the animation series produced by Bumper Films
for S4C/Channel 4 Wales and Prism Art & Design Ltd
Photographs by John Walker
All rights reserved

ISBN 1 85591 136 1

Produced and directed by Ian Frampton and John Walker
A Bumper Films Production
Printed and bound in Great Britain by BPCC Hazell Books,
Paulton and Aylesbury

TREASURE TROVE

Story by Olivia Madden
Developed from a script
by Bob Wilson

It was one of those hazy summer days when it seems a shame to stay indoors. Admirable Karia was out trimming his hedge, Sharon was getting the cafe ready for customers and Fiona and Ravi were helping Josh and Mr Laski plant birch saplings at the bottom of the field.

Each little tree was planted in its own hole with a stake to help it stand upright.

"There," said Josh, wiping his hands on his jeans. "That should do the trick."

"These trees, they grow big as your house, Ravi," said Mr Laski.

"I wish *I* lived in the country," said Fiona. "All I can see from my window is Biggot's factory."

"I'll bring you one," said Joe. "Your papa, plants it for you, maybe."

"That'll be the day," said Josh to himself.

Fiona and Ravi decided to go and pick some flowers for Fiona to take home.

"I'll give you a ride back if you like," said Josh. "I'll sit in the sun for a while. Shout when you're ready to leave."

Meanwhile, back at the warehouse, there was a good deal of banging and shouting as Spanner tried to push a large desk through the door.

"Come on, you half-wit," shouted Wilton rudely. "Get a move on. Mr Biggot asked me to get rid of that desk so that the new filing cabinets can be installed in the office."

"It's very heavy, Mr Cashmore," complained Spanner, panting with effort. "Can't I stop and have a bit of a rest?"

Spanner was lucky because just at that moment Josh and the children arrived alongside the wharf.

"Dadd-y," called Fiona. "It's me!" She jumped out of the barge and ran towards him, holding out her bunch of flowers.

"I picked them for you. And Daddy, do you know what? Mr Laski says he'll give me a tree if you'll plant it for me."

"What does he think I am?" said Wilton crossly. "An agricultural labourer? Take those flowers up to Mrs Karia to put in a vase. They're very nice, I'm sure, but I must get on. I'm a busy man, you know."

"You don't look too busy, Spanner," said Josh. "What are you up to with that desk?"

"Cashmore made me move it all on my own," moaned Spanner. "And now I've got to chop it up for firewood."

"You're kidding. A fine old desk like that? Let me have a look at it."

Josh examined the desk carefully, running his fingers over the rolltop, the drawers and the handles.

"Watch this, Ravi," he said, pressing on the inside of one of the pigeon holes.

"Gosh!" said Ravi. "It's got a secret compartment."

"I once found a gold sovereign in one of these drawers," said Josh.

"Let me look," said Ravi, all excited. He put his hand inside the compartment and wiggled it about.

"There is something here," he said, pulling out a piece of paper. "Oh, it's nothing but an old map." Ravi was disappointed.

"A map?" repeated Spanner. "What sort of map?"

"I don't know," said Ravi. "It looks dead old."
He peered at the piece of paper. "July 7th,
1864...something about a bridge..er, silver..
it's no good, I can't read the writing."

"Let me see," said Spanner excitedly.
"Perhaps there's something buried at the
bridge?" He was interrupted by the arrival
of Sharon with his mid-morning snack -
a large piece of chocolate cake.

"There you are, treasure," she said, plonking a big kiss on his cheek.

"Treasure! That's it. It's a treasure map!"

"Give it here," said Sharon. "Look, there's a diagram with a big X by Buckby Bridge. That's the bridge near my cafe."

"Hey, you're right. Come on, Sharon. If we can find the treasure, we'll be rich."

Laughing together, Sharon and Spanner ran off.

"We'd better hurry, Josh," said Ravi. "Spanner's taken the map. If we don't go, they'll find it before we do. I don't think that's fair."

"Steady on, Ravi. Real treasure seekers always do a bit of detective work first. We're going to Bapu's cottage. Jump aboard and let's go and see what we can find out."

It didn't take Sharon and Spanner long to get back to the cafe. Sharon produced a shovel and a spade and Spanner surveyed the ground to see where they should start digging. "Er, what about here, Sharon?" he said. "I'll start over there by the wall."

Sharon soon got tired of digging.

"How deep do I have to go, Spanner? Digging is dead boring, isn't it?"

"Just wait till you find that treasure, love, then it'll all be worthwhile."

Fiona and Mrs Karia had finished arranging the flowers when Fiona heard the *chug-chug* of the barge's engine. She ran out on the balcony.

"Hi," shouted Ravi. "We're going to Bapu's to look for clues. Do you want to come too?" At that moment, Wilton strode out onto the balcony. He was in a very bad temper.

"Has Spanner finished moving those cabinets yet, Jones?" he shouted.

"Well, actually..." said Josh.

"He's not at the warehouse any more," said Ravi. "He's at the cafe, Mr Cashmore."

"At the cafe!" exploded Wilton. "That's it. He's had it. Just wait till I get my hands on him," and he dashed downstairs.

"Oh, heck," said Josh. "We'd better make ourselves scarce."

At the cafe, Sharon and Spanner were still hard at work.

"Spanner, I've kept digging but all I've found is a pilchard tin. Can't I stop now?"

"No," said Spanner. "Let's look at the map again. That treasure's got to be here somewhere."

"Ooh, look out, Spanner. It's Cashmore!"

"Right," said Wilton, leaping out of his speedboat. "Just *what* is going on here?"

"I can explain, Mr Cashmore," said Spanner.

"We're digging for treasure," explained Sharon helpfully.

"Treasure!" said Wilton. "Hand over that map immediately, you idiot. You obviously aren't following the instructions."

As soon as Ravi and Josh arrived at the lock, they went up to Admirable's attic.

"Have you still got all the old canal records, Admirable?" asked Josh.

"Why, yes, They're up here, on the shelf." Josh quickly leafed through a book dated 1864, but couldn't find what he was looking for.

"What's this, Bapu?" asked Ravi, pointing to an old book propping up a table leg.

"Let's see," said Josh. He picked up the book, read through a few pages then shouted, "Ravi, you're a genius! Take a look, Admirable."

"Hm," said Admirable. "*Very* interesting."

"And now," said Josh, "I think it's time to join our friends at Sharon's cafe."

What a scene met their eyes when they arrived. The ground was full of holes and Wilton was striding about, map in hand, shouting, "Keep digging Spanner. It says 'Eleven tons of silver buried at Buckby Bridge'."

"Sorry, Mr Cashmore," said Josh, "not silver buried but silver bird. Silver Bird was a boat and she sank by the bridge."

"So there's no treasure?" cried Wilton.

"No treasure," said Josh.

Spanner looked sheepish. "Sorry about all the holes, Sharon. We've spoiled the cafe."

"Why don't we plant some of Mr Laski's little trees in them?" suggested Fiona.

"Lovely!" said Sharon. "The cafe will look right posh. All foreign and shady."

"And you'll even have your silver," teased Josh, "in the form of silver birches."

SPANNER

FAIRPORT

FIONA CASHMORE   **RAVI KARIA**